D1540738

Dagon

DAGON sounds like dragon. Dagon is only the size of your little finger nail. He came from the planet Kranton. One day his space ship broke down. It landed on earth in a big garden. Dagon soon made friends with the insects living there and decided to stay awhile.

The Wonderful Treehouse

Written by Irene Schultz
Illustrated by Ken Morton
Characters conceived by Denis Bond

Published by The Rourke Corporation, Inc., P.O. Box 711, Windermere, Florida 32786. Copyright © 1983 by The Rourke Corporation, Inc. All copyrights reserved. No part of this book may be reproduced in any form without written permission from the publisher. Printed in the United States of America.

Library of Congress Cataloging in Publication Data

Schultz, Irene, 1933-
  The wonderful treehouse.

  Summary: A disruptive student tries hard to ruin school life for the other children, but Dagon has some ideas for restoring order.
  [1. Animals—Fiction.   2. Bullies—Fiction.
3. Schools—Fiction]   I. Title.
PZ7.S3878Wo   1983   [E]   83-10939
ISBN 0-86592-877-0

THE ROURKE CORPORATION, INC.
Windermere, Florida 32786

Here is the
   school room
With Freddy
   the fly.
Walter and
   Andy
And teacher
   stand by.

Mary Moth
   loves them
And wants them
   to learn

So sometimes she
   seems to be
Angry and
   stern.

If they copy Walter
  The Wasp who acts bad,
Miss Moth makes them sorry
  That they ever had!

But one day Miss Moth
   Was just too sick to teach.
"I think I caught flu
   Yesterday at the beach."

So Captain Ant gathered
The insects about.
"Miss Moth has the flu.
She must take some time out,

So who'll be the teacher
For two days or three?"
Ernie the Earwig said,
"Please count on me."

Then Mrs. Fly warned him,
"Watch Walter because
He gets the kids doing
    The bad things he does!"

But Ernie said, "They
    Needn't do things his way!"

Here Walter is robbing
  Some candy from Ann!
He's such a big bully,
  He takes what he can!

And Walter said, "Better do
   Just what I say!
Pretend to be sleeping
   In class room today.
We sure can annoy
   Our new teacher that way!"

And they chose to follow him.
That was their fault.
There's no way that they
Could blame THAT, on Walt!

Then Ernie told Dagon . . .
   And Dag said, "Tomorrow
I'll gladly be teacher
   And they'll have real sorrow
If they think bad manners
   Are what they should borrow!"

Next morning each pupil
 Behaved like a clown
But Dag came in saying,
 "YOU JUST SIT RIGHT DOWN!"

He PILED on the work and said,
 "When you are done
The ones who are finished
 Will have all the fun."

They measured and added,
And counted and read.
They wrote and subtracted
Until Dagon said,

"You've been very good
 So we'll do something new."
But Walt said, "It's boring,"
 And stamped on Kate's shoe.

Now Dag had watched Walter
  Stepping on toes,
Smearing good paintings,
  Hitting Ann's nose.

The kids all feared Walt
  And the thought seemed to
            cheer him!
So Dag made a plan
  So the kids would not
            fear him!

"Here's a place," Dagon said.
    But Walt said, "How boring!"
Dag said, "A big tree house
    With ceiling and flooring
Is what we will build."
    Walt made noise like snoring!

But the others were thrilled!
"Oh Dagon, let's start!"
"We hardly can wait!"
"Oh Dag, you're so smart!'

"The exercise climbing
  Will make our legs strong."
"Not mine," answered Walter,
  "I'm going along,
          But you can't make me climb!
          I'm flying this time!"
So Dag strapped his wings.
  "No Walter you're wrong."

"First let's make
    some rope
To get up
    and down.
Don't use
    any grass
That is dried up
    or brown."

"I'm bored," Walter said
    With a terrible frown.

Then Dagon climbed up
  In the gooseberry plants
And fastened the rope
  Without tearing his pants.
And Walter said, "Boy,
  Will this scare you poor ants!"

From the gooseberry bush
  To a ring on the ship
The rope was stretched out.
  "OK let's start the trip!"

So they followed Dag up
   Safely tied to his waist
And they brought loads of twigs
   With wonderful haste,
All except Walter
   Who seemed made of paste.

He was so scared he stuck
  After scaring the rest!
So they all pulled him up
  To their gooseberry nest.
And they saw that he was
  Just a scared silly pest . . .

And there in the berries
  They twisted and tied
'Til they had a fine house
  They could look at with pride.

All except
  Walter
Who held on
  and cried!

The tree house was finished.
   Dag helped Walt around.
Then Dag said, "It's time
   To return to the ground."

And Walt said,
  "I bet that you kids will be scared!"
But when they were ready,
  He gulped and he stared.

Fred Fly and small Andy
  And Annie Ant too,
Said, "This was such fun we all
  Want to thank you."

But Walter just said,
  "It was boring!" and "Poo!"

And now they start down
  But they feel the rope shiver,
For Walter is frightened
  Right down to his liver!
He's ready to cry
  And his chin starts to quiver.

Once down, Dagon said,
 "The kids all can see
A bully's not brave,
 But as scared as can be.
So stop trying to frighten
 An ant or a bee,
Or Kathy, or even
 The littlest flea!"

The next morning Walter
   Was good as can be.
And Miss Moth said, "Dag,
   You have helped, I can see."
And Dag shouted . . . "If there's
   More trouble . . . call me."

DAGON SAYS. . .
"INSIDE, A BIG BULLY
   IS TERRIBLY WEAK.
IF OTHERS STAND UP TO HIM,
   OFF HE WILL SNEAK."